# Finklehopper Frog

## Irene Livingston
## Illustrations by Brian Lies

Tricycle Press
Berkeley · Toronto

Finklehopper, Finklehopper,
Finklehopper Frog
saw that all the other folks
were going out to jog.

Finklehopper whispered,
"I will buy a jogging suit.
I'll get myself a jazzy one,
a dandy one, a beaut!"

So Finkle got his hat and coat
and locked his little door,

then hopped to Mrs. Chimpanzee's. She ran a clothing store.

He checked out all the jogging suits.
A lot of them were cute.
He told her he was looking for
a really special suit!

SALE

S

ATHLETIC GARB

REALLY BIG TALL

XXL

XXXL

XXXXL

M

L

XXS

REALLY SHORT AND SMALL

She reached beneath the counter
and came up with something wild—
a suit with pink and purple dots!
And Finklehopper smiled.

SWEAT
BANDS

He touched it and he smoothed it
and he held it to his chin.
The suit was really rockin'!
"Let my jogging days begin!"

So home he hurried happy,
put the suit on right away,
and off he went to show the crowd
he'd jog with them today.

until he started wondering,

"Is this the way to jog?"

Now coming down the other way
was Itchy Flea the dog,

and Itchy nearly choked himself
from laughing at the frog!

"Finklehopper, Finklehopper,
Finklehopper Frog,
that's a stupid joggin' suit,"
said Itchy Flea the dog.

"And man, you're only hoppin'.
That is not the way to jog!"

Finklehopper sputtered
and he muttered in a fog,
"I've got my jazzy jogging suit,
and now I want to jog!"

Then Yowlereen the alley cat,
with half a bitten ear
and fur a little patchy,
came a-trotting from the rear.

"Finklehopper, Finklehopper,
Finklehopper Frog!
Your jogging suit is goofy
and you don't know how to jog!"

She gave a silly giggle
and she flipped her fuzzy tail
and off she went and hollered,
"Didja get it at a sale?"

Now Finkle's heart was heavy,
but he hoped it didn't show.

He bopped along, determined
he would never let them know.

But then a rabbit came along,
a ribbon on her head.
A-boing, a-boing, a-boing, a-boing!
And this is what she said:

"My name is Ruby Rabbit.
Hey, you're lookin' pretty cute,

a-hoppin' and a-boppin' in your hippy hoppin' suit!"

"You're calling this a hopping suit?"
said Finklehopper Frog.
And Ruby said, "Of course it is!
We hop! We never jog.

"So, Finklehopper, keep on doing
what you always do,
'cause hopping is the way to go,
the perfect way for you."

Then Finkle winked a froggy eye.
"Oh, Ruby, now I see
that everyone has special things
to do and say and be.

"We all can hop or jog or fly
or crawl or leap or run
and get to anywhere we want—

**For my mother, Clara—Irene**
**For Laurel—B.L.**

Tricycle Press
a little division of Ten Speed Press
P.O. Box 7123
Berkeley, California 94707
www.tenspeed.com

Design by Tasha Hall
Typeset in FF Bokka
The illustrations in this book
were rendered in acrylic paint.

Library of Congress Cataloging-in-Publication Data

Livingston, Irene, 1932-
Finklehopper Frog / Irene Livingston ; illustrations by Brian Lies.
    p. cm.
Summary: Finklehopper Frog's jogging style and wild jogging suit meet
with criticism until he runs into Ruby Rabbit.
[1. Running—Fiction. 2. Frogs—Fiction. 3. Rabbits—Fiction. 4. Individuality—
Fiction. 5. Stories in rhyme.] I. Lies, Brian, ill. II. Title.
PZ8.3.L748 Fi 2003
[E]—dc21
                                        2002009178

ISBN 1-58246-075-2

First printing, 2003
Printed in China

4 5 6 7 — 07 06 05 04 03